Black ink
Paper tissues
Cartridge paper
Coloured paper
Textured paper
Sketch pad

Drawing
Drawing
Drawing
Fixative s

So you want to learn to draw? First of all, you must learn to observe. Then, try to draw naturally and honestly. As you progress, your skill and knowledge will increase, and technique will come with practice and experience.

In this book you will find the simple rules necessary to make a reasonably accurate sketch of a subject: a guide to the untrained eye.

Whether you want to draw people or landscapes, here are answers to some of the basic problems you will meet in constructing your drawings.

Acknowledgments
The author and publishers would like to thank the following people for their drawings used in this book: pages 34, 35, 36/37, Frank Humphris, page 38, Hubert Williams and page 39, Chris White.

© LADYBIRD BOOKS LTD MCMLXXX

All rights reserved. No part of this publication may be reproduced, stored in a retrieval system, or transmitted in any form or by any means, electronic, mechanical, photocopying, recording or otherwise, without the prior consent of the copyright owner.

Drawing

*written and illustrated
by* KATHIE LAYFIELD

photographs by TIM CLARK

Ladybird Books Loughborough

> ### *Learning to draw is learning to see*
>
> *An essential skill of drawing is the ability to put down on paper what you are actually seeing. To achieve this skill, work your way through the book in the sequence in which it has been written.*

Using your materials

Before you draw, you need to get to know your materials. Pencils can be bought in a wide range of grades. Most of the time you will find those with a 'B' grade most useful. Do not stick to one pencil. Different qualities of line and shading can be achieved by each of these 'B' grades.

Then try to widen your range of drawing tools and experiment with them to find out the different effects you can achieve. Drawings of different types can be made using charcoal, wax crayon, pen and ink, ballpoint, fibre tip or conté crayon etc.

Line
Try with all your drawing tools to make the following lines: delicate, heavy, thin, thick, flowing, broken, woolly, smudged. Alter the pressure or the speed whilst drawing a line, and notice the effect.

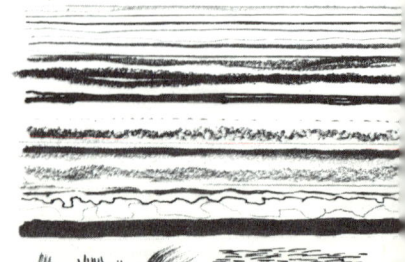

Shading
The means by which you can show light and shade can be achieved in different ways. Using your pencil to draw parallel lines close together, and altering the pressure as you do it, can give different degrees of shadow. Using lines that cross each other (cross-hatching) is particularly effective with pen and ink.

For cloudy effects you may use charcoal, or soft 5B or 6B pencils, carefully smudged with your finger. Dense shadow can be created by colouring in the area solidly, using the side of the pencil point with very firm pressure.

Sometimes you can suggest a curved surface by using curved lines. An interesting shading effect can be achieved by painstakingly using dots, as in newspaper photographs.

What to draw on

The type of paper you use will perhaps decide which drawing tool to use. Card or smooth paper is good for pen and ink work but grainy papers are more suitable for pencil and crayon work.

Coloured papers are pleasant to work on, particularly with conté crayon or charcoal. White chalk or crayon can be used to denote highlights.

Perhaps to begin with you might set up a simple *still life* group using boxes or cartons. The kitchen should provide a wealth of different shaped boxes to use. The photograph below shows an example of an ideal sort of arrangement. In this exercise we are training the eye to see accurately the shapes and sizes of the boxes and their relationship to each other. By keeping the arrangement directly in front of us, we see the boxes as flat shapes.

The grid will help you to measure the distances and proportions. It will also help you to check whether your lines are accurate, vertically and horizontally. Try not to use a ruler. Ruled lines are sometimes dull and characterless, telling little about either the character of the object you are drawing, or about you and your attitude as an artist.

If the type of drawing you want to do is that which conveys feeling, atmosphere, expression, texture or

movement, then you will need to make the most of your previous experiments with different materials. When you have chosen your subject, think very carefully about which paper and drawing tool will show best what you want to draw. Also which is the best style to show others what you saw and felt when you decided to draw this subject?

What to draw

For many centuries artists have chosen to draw the world around them, finding pleasure and interest in recording both inanimate objects and living things. Beautiful landscapes, interesting buildings, people, animals, flowers and domestic objects will continue to inspire people to draw. However, the world is full of unusual, strange and interesting corners. Sometimes the subject matter for a good drawing is very close to us. A piece of fruit or vegetable, piles of clothing, untidy cupboards, stones, weeds, broken things, scrap metal or paper, bark, shells, seaweed and thousands of other things, all show pattern, texture, shape and shadow.

Looking closely at the subject

It is important to learn how to look closely at the relationship between the shapes of objects, the shapes in between them and the lines and angles which make up these shapes. All the time you are drawing, keep looking and asking yourself questions about these proportions.

For example, here are two interesting buildings. They are just the sort of intriguing buildings you might wish to draw. The following questions are those which *you* should be asking *yourself*.

1

Picture (1)

How wide is this house in proportion to its height? Is the width half the total height? Are the horizontal sections of timbering equal? How many vertical divisions are there in each? Are the spaces between these divisions equal? What sort of angle does the roof make? Where exactly are the windows? Is the door a third of the way along the base of the house? Are the windows square or rectangular? Where is the chimney in relation to the door?

Picture (2) *(top right)*

What proportion is the height to the width of this house? Are the spaces below the windows equal to each other? Are the windows the same size? Are they central? Are they perfectly rectangular? Is the door higher than the lowest window? What is the shape of the space around the roof? What angle is the roof?

2

You can easily check relationships by using your pencil as a guide. Hold the pencil between your forefinger and thumb, extend your arm to its full length and bring the pencil between your eye and the subject.

In the diagram you will see that by lining up the top of the pencil with the top of the house and moving the thumb up the pencil until it is in line with the ground, you can soon establish the height of the house in relation to the height, width and angles of other features in the picture. Remember, whatever line you draw, to look and check before you put it down, to ensure that it relates in length and position to other angles and lines on the drawing.

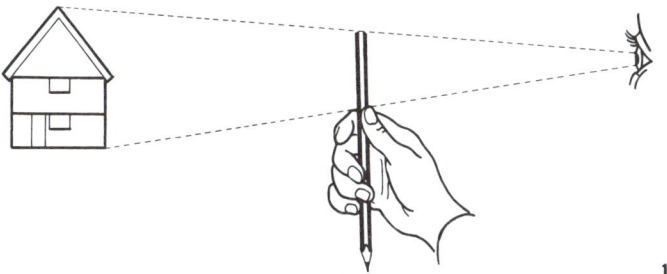

11

Plant drawing

Before you start a plant drawing, examine the plant closely. An understanding of how it grows, and its structure, will be a great help in drawing it.

Every plant has its own character too. Notice whether it is woody and strong or fine and delicate, and try to use a drawing technique to reflect this. Remember that plants are three dimensional, not flat. Some leaves or petals may project towards you or be almost hidden. You can create the impression of edges being near to you by using a darker line. Don't draw leaf veins as dark lines but shade the darker areas between them to show their pattern.

A decision you have to make before starting a drawing is what shape or size paper you should use, and which way up should it be. The important feature of your picture should fit comfortably on your piece of paper to create a well-balanced arrangement.

To help to make these decisions you could use a view-finder in the same way that a photographer does. Cut a hole in a piece of card to roughly the same shape as your paper but obviously much smaller. Hold this at arm's length, shut one eye and look through the frame you have made. Move the frame about until you can see the best composition within the frame.

The following pictures show examples of some mistakes to avoid.

In this picture the eye level is too high, so that there is too much foreground which lacks interest. At the same time the tree is too small, and does not allow you to distinguish any of the fascinating pattern and texture of the bark.

When you draw from observation you are attempting to capture the true appearance of your subject. To do this, you will have to understand the various means by which you can create a sense of depth, space and solidity.

In the picture below, you can see that by using dark tones in the foreground and gradually reducing these to become paler tones in the background, you can create the feeling of great distance. Notice also the quality of line used here. The coarse, thick use of pencil in the foreground brings it closer than the finer quality of line used for the distant parts of the scene.

Looking at light and shadow

Light falling across objects creates light and dark areas and so makes them look solid. The Italian artists of the Renaissance looked closely at this light and shadow and found that by careful use of shading and highlights, they could create what looked like solid objects on a flat piece of paper.

Three points to remember are:

1 Note the direction of the light.

2 Keep the shadows simple. Notice the strongest shapes and ignore variations, otherwise, your picture will be fussy.

3 Study the edge of the shadows.

If you stand a box on a table and light it with a torch or a table lamp, you can study the different shadows created as you move the light source around the box. Don't forget to look at the shape of the 'cast shadow' on the table top.

Now try an orange. If you look closely, you will see that the shadow is at its darkest nearest the light source where the greatest detail of the texture can be seen. Do notice that the shadow gets lighter the further it moves away from the light.

Once you have experimented in a simple way and have begun to understand light and shade,
you might enjoy drawing a picture using no outline, only areas of light and shade.

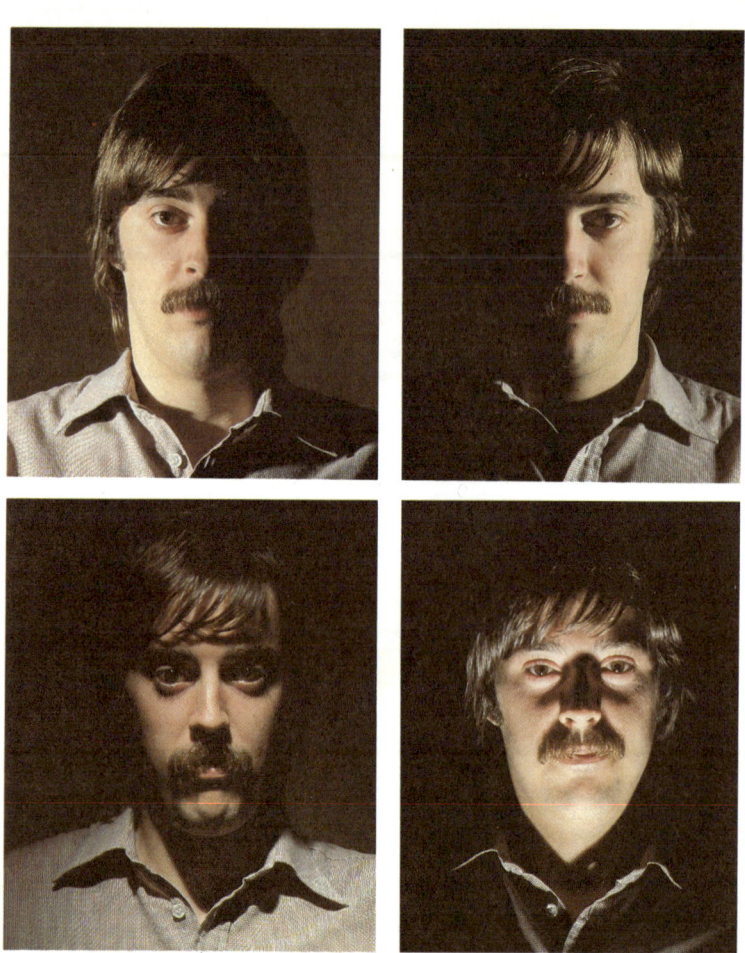

These photographs show the striking changes that occur on a head when the direction of light is altered. Before you draw a still life or a portrait, make sure you are using your lighting to the best advantage. Side lighting is usually the most successful and can be either daylight from a window or light from a reading lamp.

Drawing a portrait

Before you start to draw a portrait, look very carefully at your model. There are certain proportions you must be aware of if you are going to make a success of this work. A head is based on an egg shape with some areas receding into the egg (eye sockets) and in other places protruding (the nose). If you look at the head full-face, you will notice that quite a large area of the top of the head is visible. Faces are only part of the large egg shape. Remember that all surfaces of the human head are curved, and your drawing will depend a lot on the use of shadow. If you divide a head into three, you will find that the area of the face between the tip of the nose and the eyebrows will fit exactly into the middle third. This will help you to position these features. Once you have drawn the eyes, notice where the ears are positioned in relation to these.

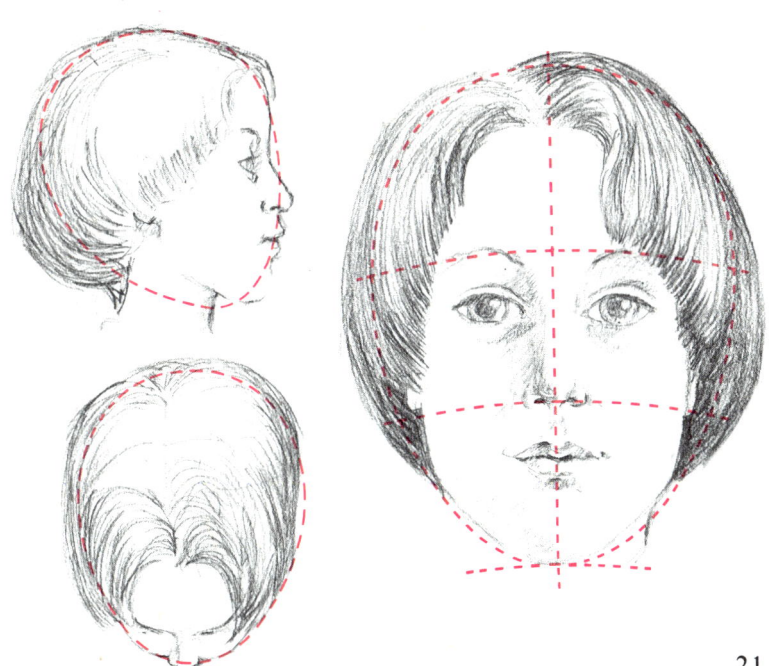

A three-quarter view of a head is more interesting, but it presents a few more problems. Remember that whatever the view, the relationship between the features remains the same. Now let us look at the head in different positions.

When the head is raised, the eyes, nose and mouth follow an upward curve. The eyes are *above* halfway, and the ears are now lower. As the head is lowered, more of the top of the head is seen and the features fit into a downward curve. The eyes are *below* halfway with the ears slightly higher. Get someone to sit for you and move their head so that you can see for yourself what happens.

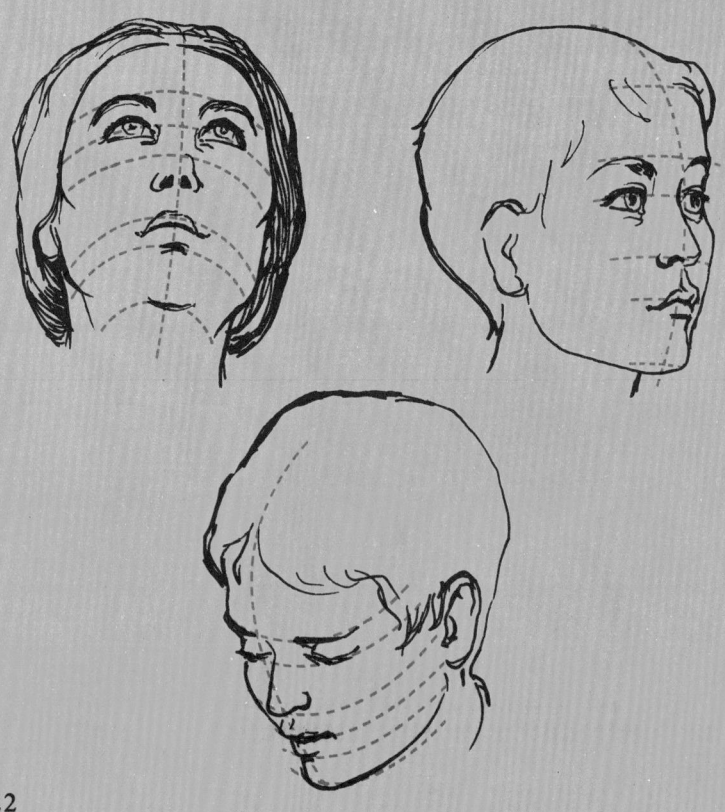

Portrait drawing detail

Once you have checked that your proportions are correct, you can start drawing the features in more detail.

Eyes are balls set deeply into sockets. Notice how eyelids mask a good deal of the eye and particularly the top part of the pupil. There is also a rounded corner on the inside of the eye near the nose. Generally, eyelashes are better shown by the use of a dark line and shadow. Only in close-up will some individual lashes actually be shown.

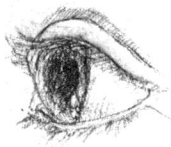

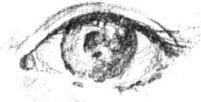

A nose is not drawn by line. It can really only be seen because of the light and shade surrounding it – except at its tip, near the nostrils.

A mouth can best be drawn by first defining the line that is the opening between the lips. The actual lips then need to be drawn by shading, the top often darker than the bottom lip. Underneath the bottom lip there is often quite a strong shadow if you are using normal side lighting.

Remember that the sides of the face curve away from you. The face does not have a hard edge, so be careful not to draw too harsh an outline. Sometimes it is possible to avoid drawing a line at all if the hair can be drawn as shading.

How people differ

The structure of the human face differs according to age, sex or nationality. Expression alters appearance, but the basic proportions always stay the same.

1. In old age the face becomes wrinkled as flesh loses its firmness.
2. Babies and young children have soft rounded features. Faces are plumper and unlined.
3. Negroid features reveal flatter broader noses, fuller lips and often a longer skull structure.
4. Oriental faces are flatter and the characteristic eyes are less deep-set than those of Westerners. It is this fullness between eyebrow and eyelid that creates the mistaken idea of slanting eyes.
5. The faces of older Arabic people may be weatherbeaten and wrinkled by the sun, particularly around the eyes.
6. American Indian faces often have a very hard and strong bone structure.
7. Fat faces reveal little bone structure but lots of folds.
8. Thin faces show up the basic skull structure.
9. Women's features are more rounded than men's.
10. Violent or extreme emotions are revealed in the face where muscles contract or expand to alter the features.

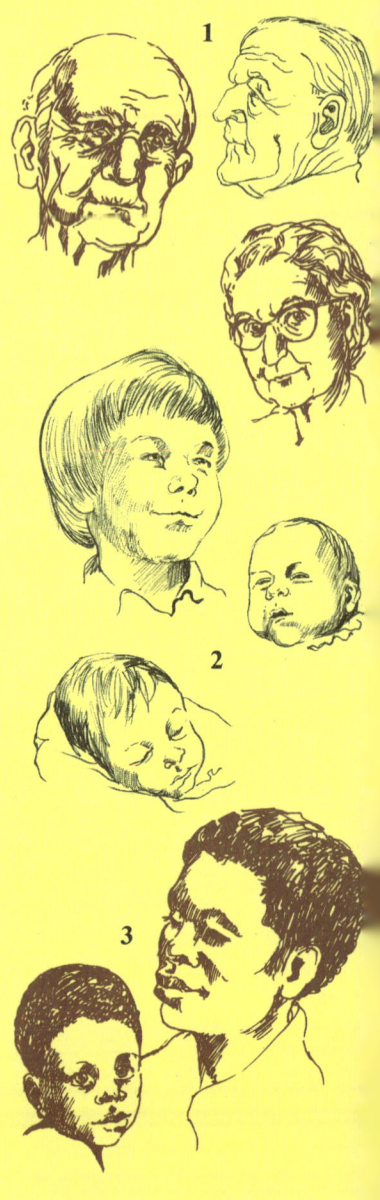

Figure drawing

Many people find figure drawing difficult and fight shy of the problem by avoiding drawing human figures. This is a pity, as figures help to put life into landscapes, give a sense of scale to pictures, and are in themselves absorbing and fascinating sources of study.

Remember that practice makes perfect! Learn to look closely, noting proportions and drawing exactly what you observe. You will soon conquer your difficulties.

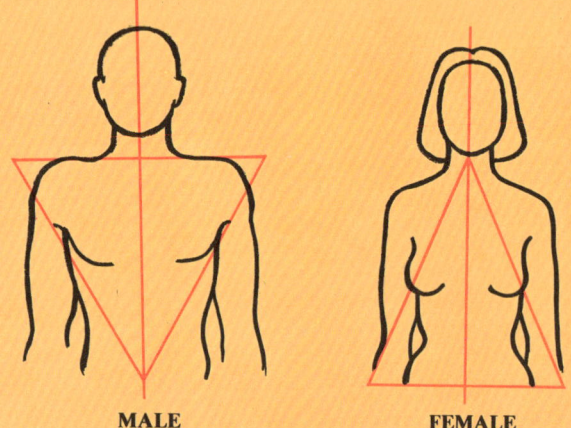

MALE   **FEMALE**

The simplest thing to notice first is that male and female forms are basically like these two diagrams.

Babies, of course, are considerably smaller than adults but notice how a child's head is proportionately larger than its body. The body grows at a much faster rate than the head.

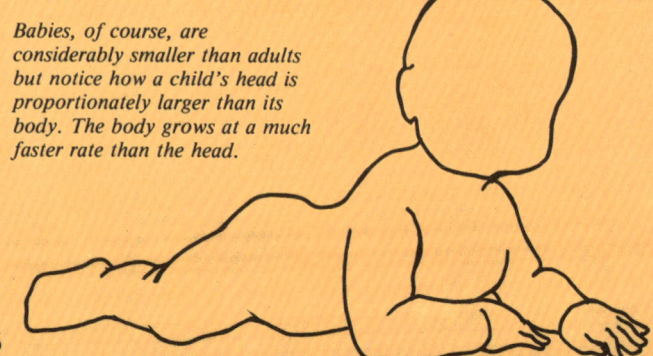

Proportions

The diagram below shows that the head and trunk make up one half of the body and the legs the other half. As a general guide, the head will go into the figure approximately seven and a half times. Men's shoulders are wider than their hips generally and the reverse is usually true for women. Of course, you must realise that every human being is different, so these rules are only guide lines.

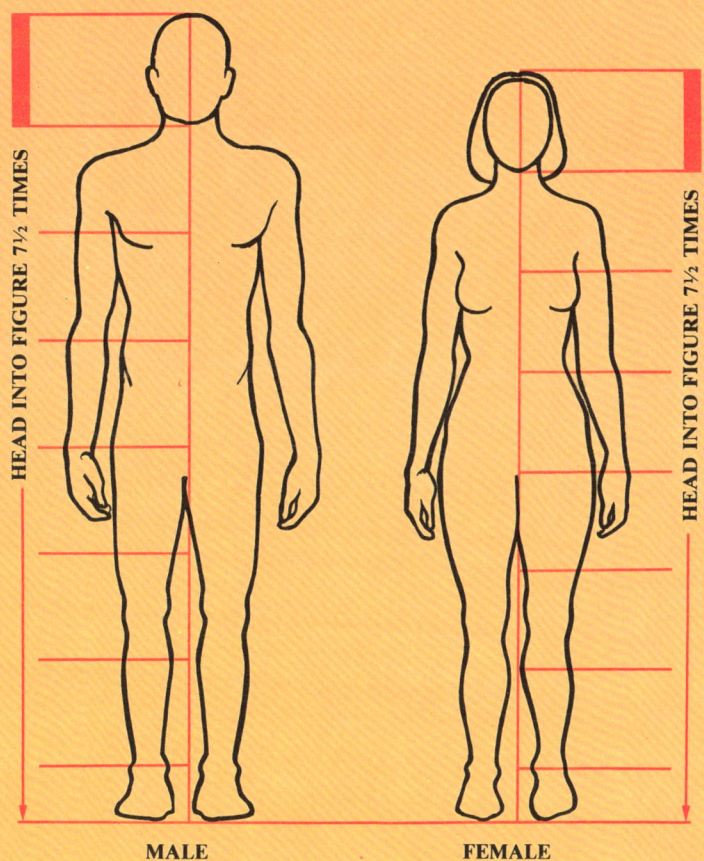

MALE   FEMALE

When you observe people you will become aware of the thousands of different positions the human body can assume. Only by constant practice will you gain confidence and accuracy but there are some points which will help you.

Whether a person is upright, sitting, or in motion, gravity demands balance. Our bodies always adjust to this balance. Even when a figure is standing with the weight on one hip, the body balances itself in order to stay upright.

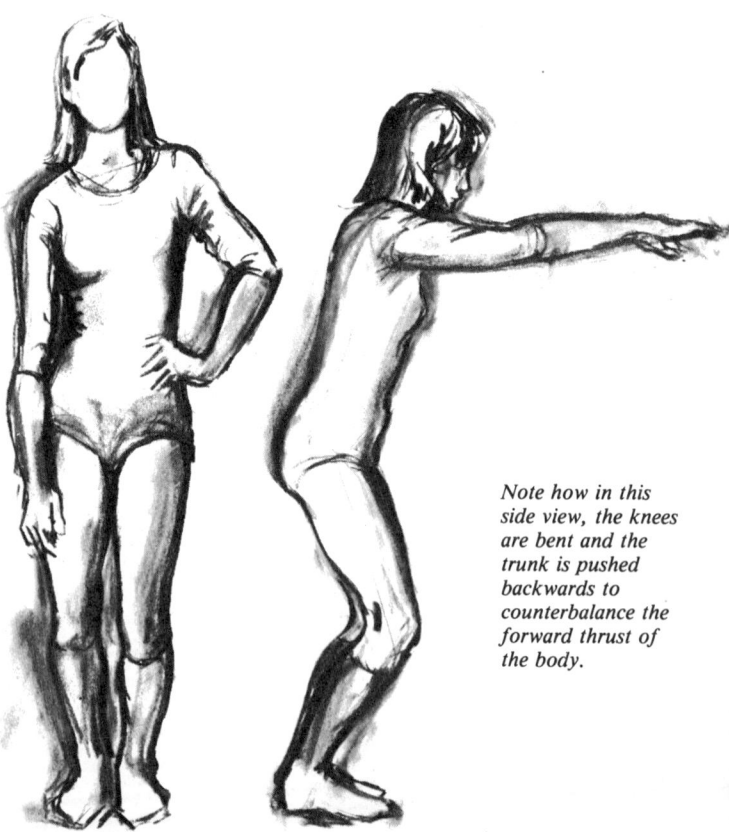

Note how in this side view, the knees are bent and the trunk is pushed backwards to counterbalance the forward thrust of the body.

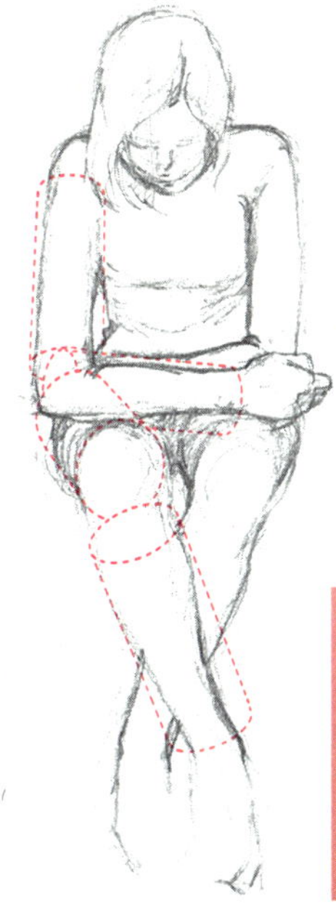

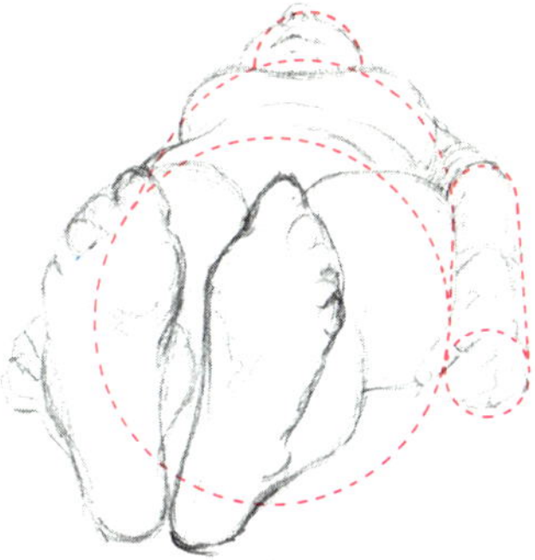

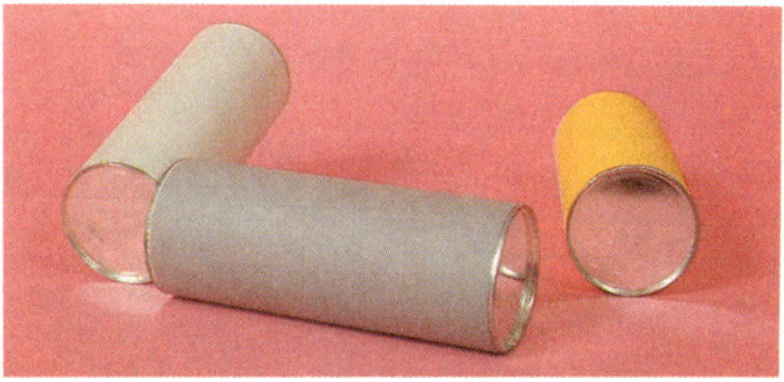

If a figure, or part of a figure, is projecting towards us the problem of *foreshortening* occurs. As the body is based on curves, the foreshortening can be understood by simplifying the shapes in question to become cylinders.

It sometimes helps to slightly enlarge the proportion of the part of the body that is projecting towards you. These hands, for example, are larger here than you might expect, but this, along with the heavier use of line, will give your figures some life.

Figures in action

A few lines are all that is necessary to capture a sense of movement. To begin with, when drawing figures that are repeating the same action, you must train your eye to discover the direction of the main lines of the action, in the body, the arms and the legs.

As you gain experience you will find that you spend more time looking and then sketching what you remember of the figure so that you can build up the information to make a complete image. Once again, you will notice how the body attempts to balance itself with arms and legs working alternately and the body tilting.

Using a sketch book to record people, whether in action, resting or working, is just as important as drawing models who have posed for you. Often the active quick sketches can be useful to you when you are composing a larger picture. In fact, a sketch book is a source of pictures of a very personal and individual nature and is the most important item of your equipment.

Clothes – what happens to them

Notice how clothing follows the curves of the human form. The collar disappears around the back of the neck and the sleeves around the arms. Observe the folds at the joints and notice how they show the form beneath as well as telling us something about the weight of the material. Light material creases more easily; heavier cloth makes broader folds. You can also suggest the texture of cloth by the way in which you use your pencils.

You will see that cloth pulls across pressure points, but then softens as it falls. It can be fascinating to study cloth through detailed drawings. Watch the way it creases when it is in motion, either in the wind or when worn by a moving figure.

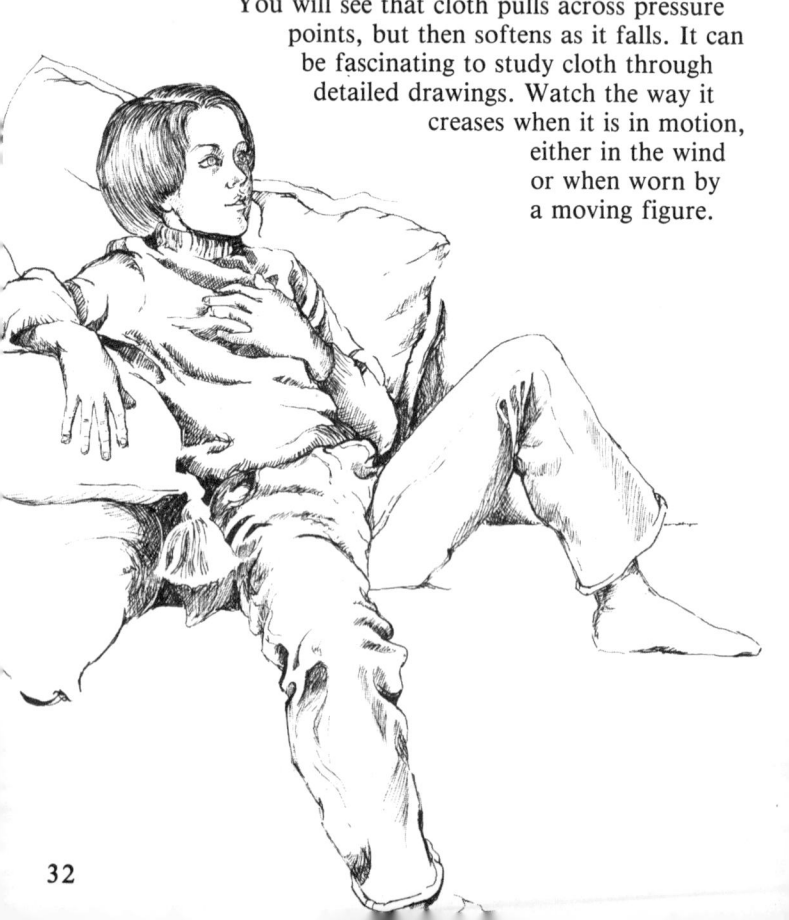

This example of a drawing of an unmade bed is a useful exercise. Once again, it will help you to understand how light and shade play a vital part in drawing clothing and material generally.

The 'anatomy' of trees

As trees play such an important part in landscape, look carefully at the different types. Look at their proportions. Study the way branches grow from the trunk. Do they grow upwards and fairly straight, or sideways with lots of curves? Don't forget that trees are three dimensional and that many branches will appear to overlap and project towards you.

Groups of trees

You can make an interesting sketch of groups of trees. Again, look for and study the general outline of the group. Select and simplify where required. Leave out any tree or bush that interferes with the overall arrangement.

A dead tree or a light coloured tree against a dark group of trees can be effective.

Learn about landscape

Sketching out of doors can be most rewarding. It will sharpen your observations. You will see things that you were not conscious of before. You must remember to select and simplify, for nature does not do it for you.

Note how details are more noticeable in the foreground and how trees and fields become simplified in shape and less distinct in detail as they recede into the distance.

This drawing was done on grey pastel paper with a black conté chalk pencil and careful use of white chalk to show the highlights.

Perspective

Another popular source for drawings is architecture. The variety of line, shape, texture and pattern in a city, town or village, or even in a simple building can make an absorbing study. There are several problems to overcome when drawing townscapes. The main one is the problem of *perspective*. That is the art of giving your picture depth and distance.

It is perspective which makes people, buildings and other things in your picture look smaller, the further away they are. A house may be much smaller than a person depending on whether it is in the foreground of your drawing or far away in the distance.

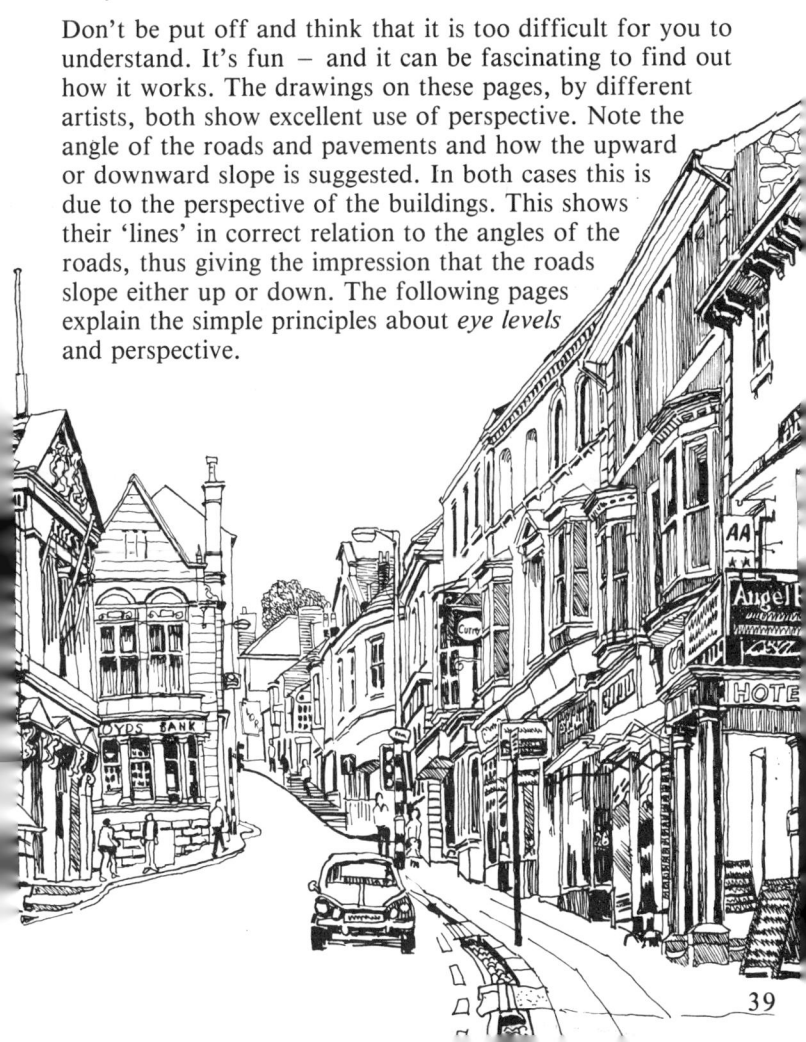

Don't be put off and think that it is too difficult for you to understand. It's fun – and it can be fascinating to find out how it works. The drawings on these pages, by different artists, both show excellent use of perspective. Note the angle of the roads and pavements and how the upward or downward slope is suggested. In both cases this is due to the perspective of the buildings. This shows their 'lines' in correct relation to the angles of the roads, thus giving the impression that the roads slope either up or down. The following pages explain the simple principles about *eye levels* and perspective.

Remember the simple rule, ALL HORIZONTAL LINES (that is, the lines of the roofs, windows and doors) MUST GO TO A VANISHING POINT on your EYE LEVEL.

The eye level is the height at which you are viewing a scene as you draw. Above, the view is from a high level. The man in the picture is looking down on the street. You will notice that all the lines marked on this picture below his eyes, run up to his high eye level.

Down at street level the man's eye level is very low, compared to the tall buildings. The lines of the buildings run down to his low eye level. Only the lines of the pavement or road run up, as they are below his eye level.

VANISHING POINT

EYE LEVEL

This illustration of a model house shows how the two sides of the building follow their own lines of perspective, to two separate vanishing points. Although there are two vanishing points they both appear on the same eye level.

When you are sketching outside, hold your pencil out in front of you and line it up with the main lines of the roof and the base of the building. This will give you a guide to

VANISHING POINT

C *EYE LEVEL*

In this inside scene you have slightly different perspective problems. With the furniture standing at different angles to each other, the perspective lines drawn through each individual piece of furniture run to their own vanishing point.

If you look closer at the illustration, you will see that the perspective lines running through the settee meet at a vanishing point A. The vanishing point of the central rectangular table, because it is almost parallel with the settee, is very close at point B. The armchair is at a totally different angle and so its vanishing point is out to the left, at point C. Again, all the vanishing points appear on the one EYE LEVEL.

these lines of perspective and the angles at which they run in relation to your eye level. You can then base your drawing on these lines.

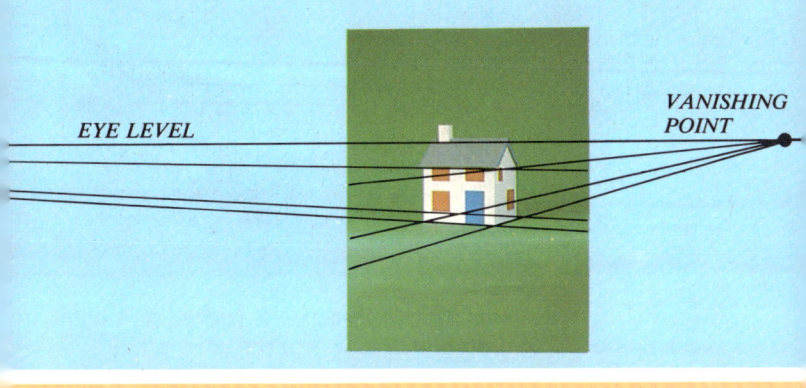

EYE LEVEL VANISHING POINT

A B

A car is full of complex curves. Imagine it packed in a tight wooden crate. The crate would give you the perspective lines and form a framework in which you can construct the main shape of the car.

The principle of the box shape or crate can be applied to many things of different sizes. Get into the habit of seeing objects within their perspective lines. Think before you draw. In this way you will train your eyes to observe things with greater accuracy, and your drawing will improve.

Each of these items is either a single basic box shape or a collection of box shapes joined together. These pictures will help you to see the important lines which you should be training yourself to see.

Ellipses

If your picture shows a car or any other vehicle, you may find it difficult to make the wheels look right. Wheels, clocks, plates or other round shapes may need to be drawn as *ellipses*. An ellipse is a circle drawn in perspective. To make this simpler, look at picture 1. This shows a can facing you and you can draw a perfect square around its circular end. If we move the can at an angle, picture 2, we must now draw a box at an angle with its lines in perspective. The circular end of the can must still fit inside the end of the box, touching all four sides. The circle is now drawn in perspective and is therefore an ellipse.

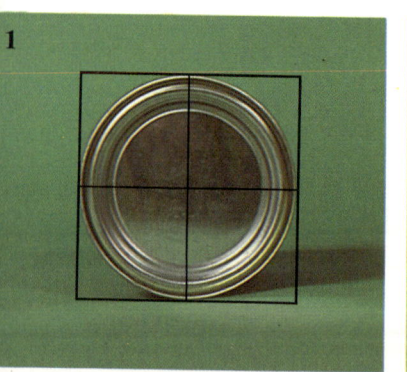

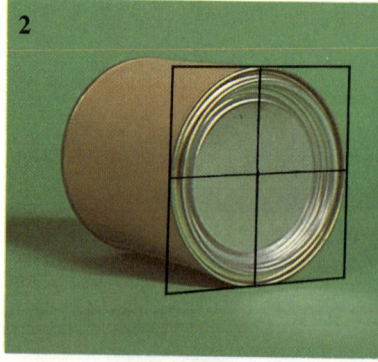

If you are drawing bicycle wheels, apply the same rules as you would when drawing a clock. When drawing car wheels, imagine that the car is driving on cans. Draw your boxes in perspective and put the cans inside. Then you can build up the rest of the car or vehicle, remembering that the lines of the bodywork will be parallel or at right angles to the ends or the sides of your boxes drawn around the cans.

Here are some objects which are based on cylindrical and other shapes. Look at the effect that light has on them. Notice especially how the shadow on the inside of an open cylinder is the reverse of the shadow on the outside of the cylinder. Lettering on objects is something that needs attention. Lettering is pattern and shape and must be drawn with as much care and observation as anything else.

Reflections

Lakes, rivers and the sea have provided inspiration for artists for centuries. You too can find pleasure in drawing water. Reflections add a new dimension to a landscape. Where water is still, reflections can be so clear that they make a mirror image as in this photograph. You will see that all vertical lines in a reflection continue into the water and an 'upside-down' image is created. Notice that reflections are darker than the scene itself.

In this photograph the reflection is still a continuation of the house. But as the house is standing a little way back from the water's edge, its reflection is cut off by the bank. See how much of the door is lost. The tree, however, growing at the water's edge, loses very little and appears to be an almost unbroken line.

Water, when moving, can be the source of very interesting patterns as the play of light creates lines and shapes that will suggest this movement and flow. Reflections still remain vertical but are lengthened, getting fainter at their furthermost points. The more you look, the more you'll understand how to portray this through drawing.

Cartoons

The art of the cartoonist is fun and it looks very quick and easy to do. In fact it requires a lot of drawing practice. Throughout this book we have talked about proportions, the relationship between shapes, lines and angles. In order to have achieved this in your drawing you will have learnt how to look very closely, to see the relevant lines and to be selective in the lines you draw. The cartoonist is even more selective. He or she will choose only a few lines to suggest a more complicated shape. Here are some examples.

Cartoons are very difficult to draw well and your time would be best spent practising all the other types of drawing in this book before even attempting them. Whatever you draw, remember the golden rule, LEARNING TO DRAW IS LEARNING TO SEE.

51

INDEX

	Page		Page
Babies	26	Perspective	38-47
Buildings	10, 11, 38, 39	Plants	12
Cars	44, 46, 47	Portraits	20-23
Cartoons	50-51	eyes	23
Choosing a subject	7, 8	mouth	23
Cloth, texture and draping	32-33	nose	23
Composition	14, 15	Proportions	10, 50
		in features	21, 24
Distance, how to create	17	in figures	26-27
Ellipses	46, 47	Reflections	49
Equipment	4-6	Relationships, checking	11, 50
Eye levels	39-43		
Faces, types of	24-25	Shading	4, 5, 12, 18, 19, 23
Figure drawing	26-32	Shadows	18, 23, 48
Foreshortening	29	Shapes, basic	6, 16, 29, 37, 48
Landscape	36-37		
Lettering	48	Sketch book as record	31
Light, direction of	18, 20, 23, 48	Still life	6, 20
Lines, types of	4	Training the eye	4, 6, 10, 12, 16, 17, 21, 23, 26, 28, 30, 32, 34-37, 44, 45, 49, 50
Mistakes to avoid	14, 15		
Paper	5, 14	Trees	14, 15, 34, 35, 49
card	5		
coloured	5	Wheels	46, 47